A Note to Parents and Caregivers:

Read-it! Joke Books are for children who are moving ahead on the amazing road to reading. These fun books support the acquisition and extension of reading skills as well as a love of books.

Published by the same company that produces *Read-it!* Readers, these books introduce the question/answer pattern that helps children expand their thinking about language structure and book formats.

When sharing a book with your child, read in short stretches, pausing often to talk about the pictures and the meaning of the book. The question/answer format works well for this purpose and provides an opportunity to talk about the language and meaning of the jokes. Have your child turn the pages and point to the pictures and familiar words. Read the story in a natural voice; have fun creating the voices of characters or emphasizing some important words. And be sure to reread favorite parts.

There is no right or wrong way to share books with children. Find time to read with your child, and pass on the legacy of literacy.

Adria F. Klein, Ph.D.
Professor Emeritus
California State University
San Bernardino, California

Managing Editor: Bob Temple
Creative Director: Terri Foley
Editors: Brenda Haugen, Nadia Higgins
Designer: John Moldstad
Page production: Picture Window Books
The illustrations in this book were prepared digitally.

Picture Window Books
5115 Excelsior Boulevard
Suite 232
Minneapolis, MN 55416
1-877-845-8392
www.picturewindowbooks.com

Printed in the United States of America.

Library of Congress Cataloging-in-Publication Data
Dahl, Michael.
Nutty neighbors : a book of knock-knock jokes / written by Michael Dahl ;
illustrated by Brian Jensen.
p. cm. — (Read-it! joke books)
ISBN 1-4048-0234-7
1. Knock-knock jokes. I. Jensen, Brian, ill. II. Title.
PN6231.K55D434 2003
818'.602—dc21
                                                                    2003004576

Nutty Neighbors

A Book of Knock-Knock Jokes

Michael Dahl • Illustrated by Brian Jensen

Reading Advisers:
Adria F. Klein, Ph.D.
Professor Emeritus, California State University
San Bernardino, California

Susan Kesselring, M.A., Literacy Educator
Rosemount-Apple Valley-Eagan (Minnesota) School District

PICTURE WINDOW BOOKS
Minneapolis, Minnesota

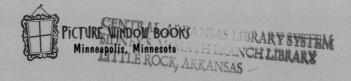

Knock knock.
  Who's there?
Justin.
  Justin who?

Justin the neighborhood
and thought I'd drop by.

Knock knock.
Who's there?
Canoe.
Canoe who?

Canoe come out
and play with me?

6

Knock knock.
    Who's there?
Noah.
    Noah who?

Noah good place to play ball?   7

Knock knock.
Who's there?
Panther.
Panther who?

Panther no panth,
I'm going thwimming!

Knock knock.
     Who's there?
Olive.
     Olive who?

Olive right next door to you.

Knock knock.
    Who's there?
Lettuce.
    Lettuce who?

Lettuce in. It's boiling out here! 11

Knock knock.
    Who's there?
Juicy.
    Juicy who?

Juicy who threw
    that snowball at me?

Knock knock.
Who's there?
Megan.
Megan who?

Megan a cake.
Do you have any eggs?

Knock knock.
    Who's there?
Amanda.
    Amanda who?

Amanda fix the refrigerator.   15

Knock knock.
Who's there?
Who.
Who who?

Do you have an owl in there? 17

Knock knock.
Who's there?
Stan.
Stan who?

Stan back. I think
I'm going to sneeze!

Knock knock.
    Who's there?
Tank.
    Tank who?

You're welcome.

Knock knock.
    Who's there?
Waiter.
    Waiter who?

Waiter minute while
    I tie my shoes!

Knock knock.
   Who's there?
Champ.
   Champ who?

Champoo your dog.
He's got fleas!

Knock knock.
    Who's there?
Freeze.
    Freeze who?

Freeze a jolly good fellow!   23

Knock knock.
Who's there?
Henrietta.
Henrietta who?

Henrietta bowl of ice cream,
and he's still hungry!